Twister
And His Adventures

Benjamin Franklin Walker

Twister and His Adventures

Copyright © July 2024 Benjamin Franklin Walker

ISBN: 978-1-953526-62-5 (Print)

ISBN: 978-1-953526-63-2 (eBook)

Published by TaylorMade Publishing, LLC

Jacksonville, FL

www.TaylorMadePublishingFL.com

(904) 323-1334

Table of Contents

Forward

Hi! My name is Twister. I know it is not a common name, but I am from the backwoods of east Texas. Follow me as I lead you on a journey of legend and reality covering different events that will shock, excite, and amuse you and will show you what life is all about.

Also, its pleasures and dangers, its pitfalls, and its enchantments. This could be your life. Think back and realize that life is always changing. This story is about Twister, his father and mother and how life was influenced and partly molded by Twister's ancestry and heritage.

Chapter 1: Adventure and Enchantment

My Pa's name was Duster, a mountain man from back in the hills and hollows of Missouri. A roaming man he was and could not seem to stay in one place very long. He roamed from one place to another desiring to know what was beyond the next hill. Duster my father lived on a farm in upper eastern Missouri. Duster was raised by God-fearing Christian parents who were peaceful, law-abiding people. My Mom was a black-eyed, tan-skinned part French and Indian girl from the "Big Thicket" outlaw land of east Texas.

Mother was the only daughter of an Indian family who lived in the caves along the upper banks of the Sabine River. She also had two brothers named Flying Eagle and Sky Hawk. Her father's name was White Claw and her mother's name was Morning Dew. My mother's name was Flower Flowing in the Breeze.

The Roaming Man

Being a restless man, my dad liked adventure. When he grew to be a man of twenty years old, Pa set out from his home on foot through the timber lands, fields and river valleys of Missouri, Tennessee, Arkansas and the enchantment of the next hill or valley drew him on. Finally, Dad came to a swampy region in the upper corner of the state of Louisiana. There dad made a "Jon Boat" or as the Cajun people call it a Perow.

Then he set out through the swamps, back waters, and bayous. After days of endless rowing, he came to a landing he later learned was named Little Cyprus. This landing is where the Sabine River flows into the Sabine Lake coming down through south Texas and the Sabine Lake eventually flows into the Gulf of Mexico right between the border of Texas and the state of Louisiana.

The Tiring Struggle

Venturing up this rugged muddy river, the bank full of the rainy season, he rowed day and night for a long weary week. Bone-tired and weak to complete exhaustion from the lack of sleep and not enough food, the strain of fighting the rushing water was taking a serious toll on his mind and body. Drawing near the bad land swamp of the Big Thicket Indian country, he then encountered the furious rapids of this southeast Texas waterway. Worn out on the barren land and starving he dragged his Perow onto a marshy bayou, struggling a few more hundred feet in search of a dryer high place.

He finally collapsed under a big oak grove and fell on his face in a deep sleep. The next day after resting a while, he made camp and laid back to rest and recover from his treacherous journey.

Chapter 2: The Beauty of Nature

While Twister was in a deep slumber, a sparkling-eyed Creo-Indian girl came upon his camp as she was searching for roots, berries, herbs, and nuts. Startled at the sight of his haggard appearance she thought this strange human was dead. The beautiful young Indian girl ran to fetch her father and brothers who were tanning hides near the cave they lived in along the high cut of the river bank a few hundred yards over through the thick brush.

Flower Flowing in the Breeze told what she had seen. The men folk gathered up their weapons and headed up the trail to see for themselves what caused the girl such commotion. As they approached the small clearing in the forest beneath the large oak trees, they saw a tattered fellow there lying stretched out on a blanket of oak leaves and pine needles.

As they approached, Duster sensed danger or an approaching foe and quickly sprang up and what a fright he gave everyone with his quick reaction. Realizing his quick movements of shock and seeing these Indians appeared friendly, he made a sign to the Indians meaning peace or friend. Puzzled by this stranger, the father White Claw and the two brothers Flying Eagle and Sky Hawk came on into the camp after Duster gave a sign inviting the father and sons into camp for a powwow or talk.

Then Duster offered the Indians a piece of dried jerky and a cold biscuit. Not knowing at this time or stage of events that this encounter would be the beginning of a true and long lasting relationship between strangers from different walks of life.

A New Day Begins

As the evening passed, White Claw invited Duster to come with them to their dwelling place where they had a dry bed made for him of leaves and pine needles covered by softly tanned raccoon hides. Duster's bed was placed near the entrance of the cave so he could feel more comfortable.

Beholding His Future

As Duster, White Claw, and the sons entered the cave, Duster stepped to one side of the cave entrance to see his surroundings. As Duster's eyes grew accustomed to the dimly lit cave, he stood in awe looking at the sight of one of the prettiest girls he had ever set eyes on in his whole life. Flower Flowing in the Breeze was standing in the shadows of the cave near a small fire there against the back wall of the cave dwelling tending a pot of food.

The smoke and odors were gently being drawn upward to an opening in the ceiling of the cave leaving a pleasant pine bark aroma mixed with the smell of bear meat cooking in the cooking pot.

Chapter 3: Opportunities In Life

In this dense wooded swamp area, there were not many opportunities in life and these two young people were brought together in such an environment and just naturally took to each other from the start.

As the days passed by Duster and Flower Flying in the Breeze grew increasingly fond of each other until the day her father White Claw showed them another cave down around the river bend about three miles.

From that time on Duster and his new bride Flower Flowing in the Breeze were together everywhere they went. He took her hunting with him, something Indians normally did not do, and when she would go gathering roots, berries, herbs, nuts, and other food to eat he would be by her side.

Chapter 4: Here Comes Twister

One bright cold spring morning they had an addition come into their lives when a little bundle of joy was born into their cave dwelling of a home. This curly haired Texas Tornado would change their lives forever. Just keeping up with him was a full-time job for both of them from the start. So, they named him Twister because he was so much like one of those destructive Texas tornadoes.

Twister would get into more trouble than any five of the other children but always found ways to cajole his way out of it just as fast. As Twister grew older, he had to begin dealing with grownups and could not con his way out of the trouble he was in so he would turn into a pure furry and bang heads and break bones until he was free and clear. Then he would head back out into the dense swamp again where few people could ever follow or find him unless he wanted them to.

Chapter 5: Living On His Own

As Twister grew older and ventured into the large cities and boom towns such as Batson Prairie, Beaumont and Port Arthur, Texas this rugged young fellow started running with the wrong crowd and became meaner as each day went by.

Eventually he started working in the oil fields with the rough and tough roughnecks that operated the drilling rigs and then he fell in love with working on the fishing boats and hanging around the fishing docks and this work became his life.

As the story goes, born in a cave along the riverbanks of the Sabine River smack dab in the swamp near the town of Nacogdoches, Texas. Twister cut his teeth on catfish line, alligator tail and such so trouble and fighting people did not bother him much. As days went by and the swamp dried up of which also caused quite a furry for more outlaws and roughens were forced and drawn to the boat docks and fishing piers and trouble grew worse every day.

The Jury

That is part of the reason the courts called you men here today for this jury duty. You that knew Twister was sought out to witness this trial and see justice conducted. My Pa was a mountain man from back in the hills and hollows of Missouri. He, being a rambling man, could not stay in one place and always needed to see what was over the next hill.

He roamed from one place to another, from Missouri to Tennessee to Arkansas and Louisiana and then into the bad lands of Southeast Texas, where he met up with my mother. I was raised on razor back hog meat and grizzly bear fat, wrestling gators and chasing black panthers in the back swamps. Just like a Texas twister tornado that I was named after, that is how I grew up.

I have fought the best and the worst, the meanest and the ugliest, but now I have some reckoning to do with the law that has finally caught up with me and my rampaging ways. I am having to reckon with my uncontrollable temper and hateful spirit that got me into this mess. Now I will have to rely on the honesty and forgiving nature of this court and jury to consider my charges and see that sure justice is carried out.

I know no one nor have no one to plead my case for me so I place myself at the mercy of the court and jury. In the midst of my growing up here on the boat docks and backstreets. I have shot, knifed, bit ears off the men I was fighting, breaking arms and legs, knocking out teeth and terrible things to do for survival. Not only that, but I knocked men out, pushed them in the lake, gigged them in the side and mangled their brains.

I am guilty of so much I do not know how I could ever go free. Even though I have had a life changing experience with the Lord Jesus Christ, no one will know me from this time on because I am not the same person that I used to be because of the change the Lord made in me.

Twister's Epitaph (Or Defense If You May)

Do what you will. I will be at peace with the results because, that raging torrent that lived within me has been overcome forever. I have met the Master; the Lord Jesus Christ; and my life was transformed. From this moment my life will be different for the Master's sake.

Thank you and carry on with your responsibility and duties. This epitaph was placed on the Twister's gravestone years later:

"TWISTER THE TORNADO"

About the Author

Benjamin Franklin Walker is a Messenger for the Lord since July 12, 1947, when he was saved at an 8-week camp meeting revival in Green, Texas. He was later baptized in the San Antonio River. Ben has been a great street witness with a multitude of gospel tracts and being a living testimony wherever he happens to go. Ben has a true and extensive testimony which would make a large book!

Currently, Brother Ben is focusing on the present and into the future as a Valiant Christian. Ben is proclaiming and standing on God's commandments, which are His standards, instructions, and statues forever more.

During Ben's time on various ships, he collaborated with chaplains conducting Bible studies and Sunday services. He has been associated with vast number Christians organizations in his worldly travels.

Ben has been an asset to Mission Harvest America for years serving with Dr Dewey Painter. He is a member in good standing with the International

Educational Professional Accreditation Association in Jacksonville, Florida (IEPAA). Ben is currently associated with Dr. Ken Lierle, International President of Taongi National University, Jacksonville, Florida, and Liberia.

[14]

9 781953 526625